To my daddy, whose stories about the preachán
and the bodach were the best, and
to Martha for changing my life, with love Anna
To Marion, and the magnificent Milroys, with love Ros

First published in the UK in 2009 by
Alanna Books
46 Chalvey Road East,
Slough, Berkshire, SL1 2LR
www.alannabooks.com

ISBN: 978-0-9551998-5-1

Printed and bound in China

Lulu Loves Stories

Anna McQuinn

Illustrated by Rosalind Beardshaw

ALANNA BOOKS

On Saturdays, Lulu's daddy takes her to the library.

The library is VERY busy on Saturdays,

but Lulu still finds some excellent books.

When they come home,
Lulu's daddy reads
the first story.

It's about a fabulous fairy princess!

All the next day,
Lulu is a fairy princess.

She has a magical dress
and a sparkly crown.

She's just fabulous!

On Sunday night, Lulu and her mummy read the next story. It's about an amazing journey.

All day Monday, Lulu takes her friends on fantastic trips to exotic places like Paris and Lagos.

On Tuesday, Lulu chooses a
story about friends.

All afternoon, she and Ben play cafés with their babies. Lulu has cappuccino and her baby has juice.

Tuesday night, Lulu's mummy
reads a story about fierce tigers!

Next day, Lulu chases her friend
Orla all over the jungle.

Wednesday night, Lulu reads a story
about Old MacDonald and
all next day, she is a farmer.
Taking care of the animals
is tough work!

Lulu's cow is sick!

Luckily mummy knows
how to make her better.

Thursday night, Lulu and her daddy read about building.

Next day, Lulu has to fix up her house.
She needs a hammer, a saw...
and a little help from daddy.

Friday night, Lulu's daddy makes up
a story about a little girl who
has a magic pair of shoes.
Next day, Lulu's shoes
are truly magical.

They sparkle all the way
to the library...

...and all the way home.

They even sparkle while her daddy reads her a story about a wild and wicked monster!

What will Lulu be tomorrow?

More great stories from ALANNA BOOKS...
You can see all the books on line at www.alannabooks.com

Lulu Loves the Library
Hardcover ISBN: 978-0-9551998-0-6

The first Lulu book is set to become a classic and
is still available in hardcover.

Lulu Loves the Library
Paperback with multi-language CD   ISBN: 978-0-9551998-2-0

The whole story is told in the following languages:
English, Welsh, Irish, French, Polish, Italian, Turkish, Gujerati,
Urdu, Ndebele, Luganda, Igbo, Arabic, Somali, Amharic, Tigryna,
Portuguese, Spanish, and Mandarin.
You can sing along to Twinkle Twinkle Little Star at the end.

Lulu Loves the Library
Board book ISBN: 978-0-9551998-7-5

Lulu is also available with a shorter text, perfect for toddlers.

Little Frog
Paperback ISBN: 978-0-9551998-6-8

When Little Frog drops into the lives of a very normal family
chaos ensues. The family want to love him,
the trouble is, he is actually very VERY naughty...

A tremendously funny book -
underneath the hilarious story there's a warm and important
message about acceptance and belonging.

My Friend Jamal HB ISBN: 978-0-9551998-1-3
My Friend Amy HB ISBN: 978-0-9551998-3-7

These two stories describe the powerful friendships between
children from different cultural backgrounds.
Growing up together – here in a modern, urban,
multi-cultural environment – they have lots in common.
The emphasis throughout is on shared experience
rather than on difference, and the stories celebrate
how well the children get along.
Log on to: www.alannabooks.com
for SchoolsWeb pages with information
on all the issues rasied in the books.